Run for Your Life

Jack Gabolinscy

Jeremy Ley

Run for Your Life

Text: Jack Gabolinscy
Illustrations: Jeremy Ley
Design: James Lowe
Series design: James Lowe
Production controller: Lisa Porter
Reprint: Siew Han Ong

Fast Forward Independent Texts
Level 22

ISBN 978 0 17 017990 4
ISBN 978 0 17 017899 0 (set)

Cengage Learning Australia
Level 7, 80 Dorcas Street
South Melbourne, Victoria Australia 3205
Phone: 1300 790 853

Cengage Learning New Zealand
Unit 4B Rosedale Office Park
331 Rosedale Road, Albany, North Shore NZ 0632
Phone: 0508 635 766

For learning solutions, visit **cengage.com.au**

Printed in Australia by Ligare Pty Ltd
3 4 5 6 7 26 25 24 23 22

Run for Your Life

Jack Gabolinscy
Jeremy Ley

Contents

Chapter 1	Smoke	4
Chapter 2	London Bridge	8
Chapter 3	Dark Streets	16
Chapter 4	Fleet River	18
Chapter 5	Firebreak	20
Chapter 6	From the Ashes	22

CHAPTER 1

Smoke

Billy Miller woke up early
on Sunday morning, coughing.
His throat was dry and
there was a strange smell
in the room.

Billy rubbed his stinging eyes,
sat up and peered into the darkness.

Suddenly, he recognised the smell.
Smoke!

The house was on fire!

"Help!" he yelled, running for the door.
"Mother! The house is on fire!"

Then Billy remembered
that his mother wasn't home.
She was still working
at the big house near Pudding Lane.

Halfway to the door,
Billy remembered
his little sister, Elizabeth.
He turned back for her.

"What's happening?" Elizabeth called from the darkness.
"I can't breathe."

"Come! Quickly!" Billy shouted, grabbing her hand.
"The house is on fire."

Down the stairs and out the door, into Fish Street they raced.

Billy soon realised that it wasn't
their building on fire,
but one behind them on Pudding Lane.

But the fire was spreading…

The street was crowded.
People were heading towards
London Bridge to escape the fire.
Many were shouting and crying.

CHAPTER 2

London Bridge

The sky glowed red.
Thick smoke filled the air.

Gun-powder in the stores
exploded loudly.
Timber and hot ashes
blew into the sky.

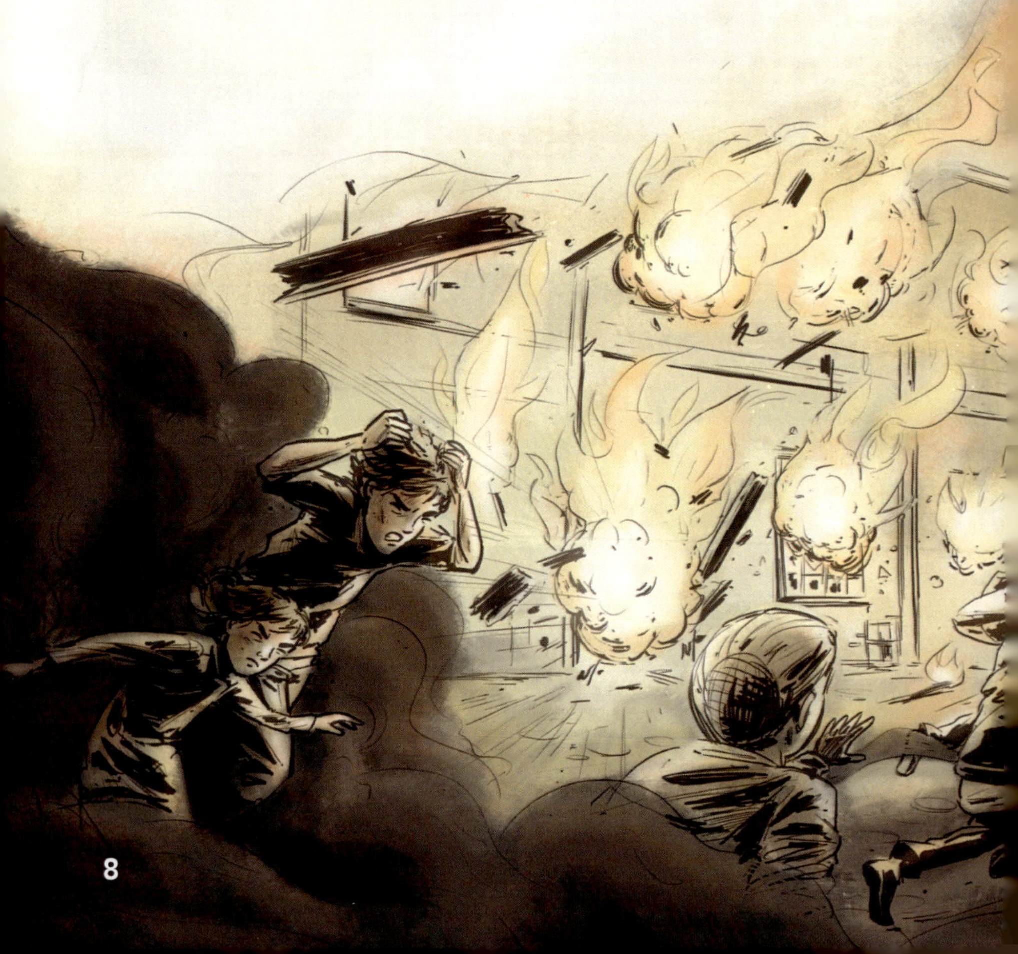

Billy couldn't decide whether or not
to wait for their mother.

Billy wished
that their father was there,
but he'd died of the plague
the year before.

Suddenly, Billy's decision was made for him. The fire jumped from Pudding Lane to Fish Street.

"Run," coughed Billy. "Run for your life!" They raced towards London Bridge. Hungry flames licked at their heels as they ran.

Elizabeth started falling behind.

“Hurry!” Billy called.
“We’ll be safe once we cross London Bridge.
It’s too dangerous here.”

But Billy was wrong –
they couldn't cross the bridge.
It was on fire.

They couldn't even turn back,
because the fire was behind them.

On they ran.
Then Elizabeth's legs collapsed.
She fell to the ground.

"I can't run anymore.
My legs hurt," she cried.

A strong wind fanned the flames.

Just as the two walls of fire
caught up to them,
Billy scooped Elizabeth up.
He turned into Fleet Street
and ran on and on.

"You can stop running," shouted a man, looking back towards London Bridge. "The fire won't come this far."

The children found a quiet alley.
"Go to sleep," Billy said.
"Tomorrow we will look for Mother."

The children slept until midday
the following day.

Dark Streets

Elizabeth woke up first.
Her throat was dry
and she couldn't breathe properly.
Clouds of smoke surrounded them
and hot ash rained down.

"Billy! Billy!" she screamed.
"The fire has come!"

Billy woke. He saw the flames.
"Run!" he yelled.
"Run for your life!"

They ran through the crowded streets
of fleeing people.

"Hold my hand. I don't want to lose you,"
Billy said.

Then Billy thought he saw their mother.
He rushed towards her,
grabbing her arm.

"Mother?" he asked.
The woman turned around and stared.
It was not her.

"I'm sorry," he said, disappointed.

The children continued on.

Fleet River

On Tuesday, Billy and Elizabeth
ran across a bridge over the Fleet River.
They stopped on the river bank to rest.

"Now we really are safe," Billy said.
"It's only a small river,
but the fire can't get over it."

Grey-black smoke clouds rose over London.
The whole city appeared to be on fire.

They found an empty church
to stay in for the night.

"Will we see Mother again?" Elizabeth asked.

Billy didn't know the answer.

During the night,
the fire leapt over Fleet River.

The children woke.
They saw swirls of smoke
coming from the church's roof.

Luckily, they noticed a side door.
They escaped just in time
to see the church go up in flames
and the roof start to collapse.

All day Wednesday,
they ran through the narrow streets
of London, looking for safety.

Firebreak

Late on Wednesday,
the children heard some explosions nearby.

To stop the fire from spreading,
the king's soldiers had been ordered
to make a firebreak.

They blew up the burnt buildings
and dragged the timber away,
so there was nothing left
for the fire to burn.

Slowly, the flames died down.

Only the smell of smoke,
and the sight of thousands
of burnt houses
and other buildings remained.
Much of the city had been destroyed.

CHAPTER 6

From the Ashes

On Thursday morning,
Billy and Elizabeth returned to Fish Street.
Their home had been
destroyed by the fire.

Nothing but ash, a burnt cooking pot
and some bricks remained.
Billy squeezed Elizabeth's hand.

"We'll find Mother," he said.
"She'll know what to do."

They set off towards Pudding Lane.

Just as they left,
the children saw a woman nearby.

She looked filthy and
her clothes were covered in ash.
She looked up.

"Billy?! Elizabeth?!" she cried.

The children ran to their mother.
She hugged them tightly.

"You're both safe!" she cried.

"But our house is gone," Billy said, sadly.

Their mother thought for a minute.

"We'll go to Uncle Henry's place
in the country," she said.
"We'll stay there
until we decide what to do."

The family left the devastated city behind.
Each of them was glad to have
the other two by their side.